GARGOYLES' CHRISTMAS

by
Louisa Campbell

illustrated by
Bridget Starr Taylor

GIBBS·SMITH
⇥P
PUBLISHER

SALT LAKE CITY

First edition
97 96 95 94 6 5 4 3 2 1

Text copyright © 1994 by Louisa Campbell
Illustration copyright © 1994 by Bridget Starr Taylor

This is a Peregrine Smith Book, published by
Gibbs Smith, Publisher
P.O. Box 667
Layton, Utah 84041

Design by Leesha Gibby Jones
Dawn Valentine Hadlock, Editor

Printed and bound in Hong Kong

Library of Congress Cataloging-in-Publication Data

Campbell, Louisa.
    Gargoyles' Christmas / written by Louisa Campbell ; illustrated by Bridget Starr Taylor.
        p. cm.
    Summary: Soured on Christmas, three New York City gargoyles begin to change their mind about the
holiday after Santa Claus helps them out of a mess of their own making.
        ISBN 0-87905-587-1
        [1. Gargoyles- -Fiction. 2. Santa Claus- -Fiction. 3. Christmas- -Fiction. 4. New York (N.Y.)- -Fiction.]
    I. Taylor, Bridget Starr.
1959- ill. II. Title.
PZ7.C15515Gar 1994
[E]- -dc20
                                                                            94-4035
                                                                            CIP
                                                                            AC

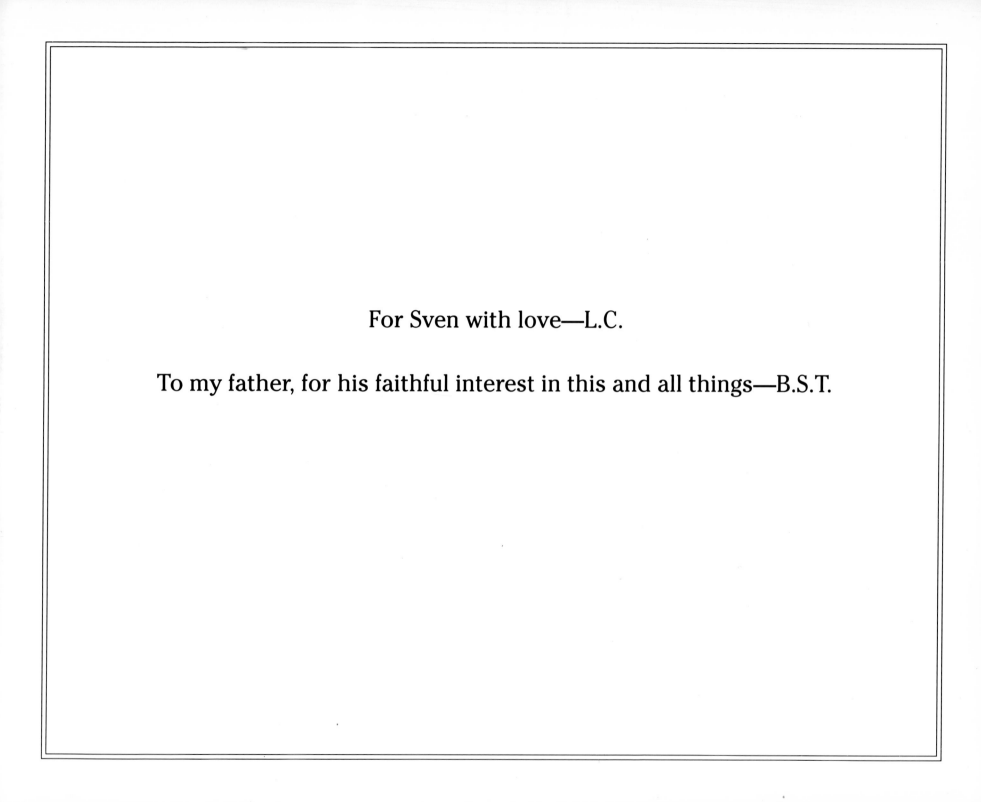

For Sven with love—L.C.

To my father, for his faithful interest in this and all things—B.S.T.

Craig, Cliff and Christabel were gargoyles carved of stone. They sat perched atop the Griffin Building on New York's Fifth Avenue. With scorn and joy the three gargoyles peered down at the concrete, the cars and the crowds. "This city is as mean and ugly as we," thought Craig. "Marvelous!"

Most of the day the gargoyles kept such gruff thoughts to themselves, locked inside their cramped, crouched bodies. But at the deepest darkest center of each night their voices were loosed from the stone and the three would chat.

I t was a delightful rush hour this evening, was it not?" chortled Craig. "The noise of the traffic was simply deafening!"

"Noise is nothing," hissed Christabel. "Lovely, grimy soot—that's something. And tonight's soot was thick as soup! Yum, yum!"

Each night the gargoyles yammered on until the black sky began to grey, and dawn light slithered down the skyscrapers. Then the gargoyles were silent once more, until the deepest darkest center of the night was upon them again.

Most of the year Craig, Cliff and Christabel were very happy in the noisy, dirty city—most of the year, that is, except at Christmas.

At Christmastime festive lights and trimmings transformed the dingy buildings and streets. A large Santa Claus decoration was rigged on the roof of the hotel across the way. The roar of the traffic was brightened by piped-in Christmas music. The jostling crowd seemed happier and at times even polite. To the gargoyles all this holiday cheer was disgusting.

One evening before Christmas, not long ago, something happened which had never happened before. Someone plopped a Christmas wreath around Craig's neck. The wreath was tied with a pretty red bow. Its pine branches smelled fresh and sweet.

R evolting!" sniffed Craig. "Horrid!" griped Cliff. "Nauseating!" raved Christabel.

The gargoyles despised the Christmas wreath. Indeed it made them so angry that they came alive with rage. Although it was long before the deepest darkest center of the night, the three could talk. In fact, the gargoyles could move their feet for the very first time in their lives.

Christabel twirled. Cliff hopped. Craig ripped the wreath from his neck and hurled it through the air. "Take that, wreath!" he growled. "Christmas-smishmas!" yelled Christabel.

Now that they were free, the gargoyles were frenzied with joy. They scampered through the window into the building. There, smack in front of their eyes, was a small Christmas tree.

"Despicable!" ranted Cliff as he smashed and tore at the tree. The desks, computers and carpets were soon littered with bits of pine and tinsel and shards of smashed ornaments. "Ha, ha!" laughed Craig.

Christabel cried, "Down! Down to the street!"

The gargoyles raged on, having a fabulous time, shrieking and flailing their arms and wings, tumbling down the stairs and out the door. They splashed into a nearby reflecting pool, which was crowned with a circle of giant gingerbread men and stripey candy canes. The gargoyles tugged and pulled at the Christmas decorations and dragged them down into the icy water.

Next the gargoyles trampled over to a department store. Lining the entrance was a row of potted spruces strung with colored lights. The gargoyles snatched and tore at the lights with such gusto that they soon became snared in the flickering bulbs. The more they struggled, the more entangled they became.

"I cannot move. I am stuck," groaned Craig. "We are helpless. We are done for."

Then Cliff wailed, "I miss my pedestal!"

"Oh shut up!" snapped Christabel. "Grow up and be a gargoyle and get us out of this mess."

The gargoyles' wails were interrupted by the clatter of hooves on pavement. "Whoa now, reindeer, whoa!" a jolly voice called. "Ho, ho, ho! You gargoyles are in a bit of a fix!"

Standing beside them was Santa Claus with his reindeer and sleigh! The Santa display from the roof of the hotel had come alive!

Christabel saw Santa Claus and spat, "P-too-ey! Why don't you mind your own business you meddling fatso!?"

"Well, now," said Santa, "we've come to help . . . but of course, if you don't want our help, we can easily go away."

Craig blurted out, "No, Santa, please do not leave us now!" Then Craig lowered his voice and said to Christabel, "Control yourself for once! Can you not see that Santa Claus is our only hope? Do you want to be stuck here like ridiculous gargoyle Christmas trees?"

"No," she admitted sullenly.

"Use your brain then!" pleaded Cliff. "If we don't get back to our pedestals before dawn, we'll turn to stone, stuck here among the humans." He sighed with despair. "The good gargoyle life will be lost to us forever."

Then, raising his voice, Craig addressed Santa, "Thank you, sir. We surrender to your aid."

S anta answered, "Yes, yes, but first you gargoyles must understand that I'll help you only on one condition." Wagging his finger, he continued, "Once you're free, you must put each and every one of these Christmas decorations back together again!"

"Never!" growled Christabel.

"Excuse her, Santa, I beg of you," cried Craig. "She does not know what she is saying."

"We'll do anything you want!" yowled Cliff. "Untangle us, please!"

"All right," said Santa, "since I have your word." Santa started his delicate work. The reindeer helped by nuzzling the strands of lights away with their snouts. As the gargoyles were freed, they felt the energy flow back into their bodies and they shimmied with the thrill.

C raig and Cliff still hated the idea of Christmas decorations, but they were gargoyles of their word. Slowly they began to help Santa tidy up. Christabel, however, stomped off to sulk and pout.

At first Cliff moved slowly, but soon he began to skip around the potted spruces as he sang a little ditty.

> *Gargoyles, gargoyles, gargoyles are we,*
> *It's quite odd that we should trim a tree,*
> *Dee-dee, dee-dee, dee-dee, DEEEEEEE!*

Craig joined in. The two gargoyles wove in and out of the potted spruces, jigging and whooping. Christabel snorted and sputtered, "Stupid gargoyles!" But despite herself, her voice sounded a bit softer than before.

Once the trees were trimmed, Craig and Cliff scurried over to the reflecting pool. They jumped in, feet first, splashed at each other and sang:

Gargoyles, gargoyles, gargoyles are we,
Splish-splash-splish, together you and me,
Dee-dee, dee-dee, dee-dee, DEEEEEEE!

Christabel could resist no longer. Into the pool she plunged. The gargoyles ducked and dived and flung water at each other with great glee. Finally the three collapsed, laughing so hard that their happy tears flowed into the frigid water.

Then all three gargoyles set to work together. Craig righted a giant gingerbread man and muttered, "Not bad, not bad at all."

"Kind of cute," added Cliff, as he propped up a stripey candy cane.

Even Christabel continued the cleanup without complaining, and soon the reflecting pool was crowned with Christmas decorations once again.

As they finished up, Santa looked at his watch and squinted at the sky. "It's not long until first light," he said. "We must be off to our post. Merry Christmas, gargoyles!"

Cliff saluted Santa, and Craig was about to say, "Merry Christmas," but a withering glance from Christabel silenced him.

Yet Christabel, along with the others, was awed as she watched Santa and his reindeer take off and fly up through the air. Although she would never admit it to herself, she was sorry to see Santa go.

T hen the gargoyles bumbled up the stairs. They propped up the office Christmas tree and tidied the litter as best they could. The three scrambled back through the window just as the black sky began to grey, and dawn light slithered down the skyscrapers.

That day Craig, Cliff and Christabel were happy to be back safe and solid on their pedestals. Rush hour was still just as they liked it—nasty and noisy and sooty. They realized that Christmas wasn't *so* terrible. In fact, it was tolerable. The gargoyles didn't even mind seeing Santa, the reindeer, and the Christmas sleigh across the way.

It was still the Christmas season, so it wasn't very long before something wonderful happened once again. Someone plopped a Santa Claus hat on each of the gargoyles' heads. Strangely enough, not one of them minded sporting that cheery Santa cap. After their caper, Craig, Cliff and even Christabel had begun to think well of Santa. The gargoyles sat thinking such friendly, happy thoughts. Although it was long before the deepest darkest center of the night, their lips loosened, words began to form in their throats, and the gargoyles felt life stirring in their fingers, toes and bellies…